A Special Birthday

COLONEL WALKER SCHOOL

Written by Kim Newlove • Illustrated by Keiko Narahashi

In an old white house over the fence from Nathan's lived Grandma Korolek. She wasn't really Nathan's grandma, but everyone on the street had always called her Grandma Korolek.

"How old is Grandma Korolek?" Nathan asked his mom and dad.

"She's older than that old house of hers," said his mom.

"She's as old as a turtle," said his dad.

"But how many years old is she?" asked Nathan.

His mom and dad didn't know.

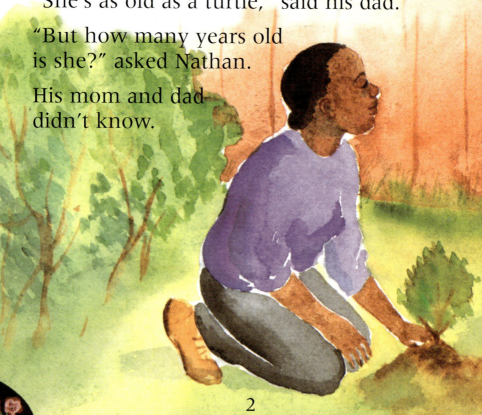

Nathan liked to take Grandma Korolek for walks. Sometimes he told her about funny things that had happened at school. Grandma Korolek always listened and smiled. She liked Nathan's stories.

"How old are you?" Nathan asked her one day

"Guess," said Grandma Korolek.

"Mom says you're older than that old house of yours, and Dad says you're older than a turtle," said Nathan.

Grandma Korolek smiled. "I am older than my house, and I guess I am older than some turtles."

"But how many years old are you?" asked Nathan. "I'm seven, and in August I'll be eight. Mom says I can have a cake with eight candles, and she says I can ask eight friends to my party. Now, how many years old are *you*, Grandma Korolek?"

"Ninety-nine," said Grandma Korolek. "On my birthday next Saturday, I'll be…"

"One hundred years old!" said Nathan.

"I can hardly believe it," said Grandma Korolek. "I remember *my* eighth birthday. My dad rented a pony so that my friends and I could have pony rides. My mom baked a big white cake with pink roses on it."

Nathan smiled. "This year you can have one hundred candles on your cake, Grandma Korolek. And you can ask one hundred friends to your party."

Grandma Korolek looked at him sadly. "I haven't had a birthday party for years, Nathan. Most of my friends are gone."

"I'm still here, " said Nathan. "I'm your friend."

Grandma Korolek threw her arms around Nathan. She started to cry. Nathan could feel her tears on his cheek.

"Grandma Korolek, you're my best friend," he whispered.

"And you're *my* best friend, Nathan!" she whispered.

"Grandma Korolek is going to be one hundred years old next Saturday," Nathan told his dad and mom that evening. "Can we have a surprise party for her?"

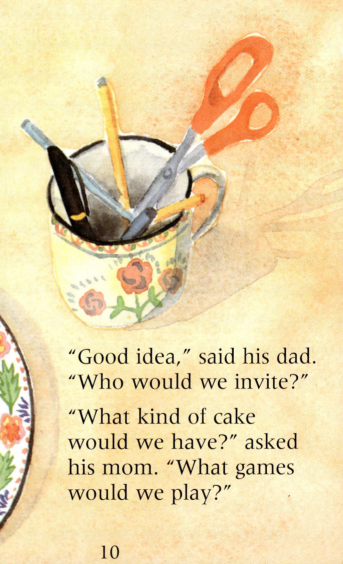

"Good idea," said his dad. "Who would we invite?"

"What kind of cake would we have?" asked his mom. "What games would we play?"

Next morning, Nathan and his dad and mom talked about the party again. Nathan made a list of their plans.

Monday
Talk to Bart, the baker

Tuesday
Call Grandma Pearson at the farm

Wednesday
See Mr. Gordon at the grocery store

Thursday
Visit Aunt Hazel at band practice

Friday
See Miss Hossip at the newspaper

Just after lunch on Saturday, Grandma Korolek heard a knock at her door. "Would you like to go for a birthday walk in the park?" asked Nathan.

"I'd love to," answered Grandma Korolek.

Nathan wheeled her into the park. "Oh, my!" she gasped, looking around.

"Look at all the people who came to your birthday party, Grandma Korolek," said Nathan.

"My, oh, my!" said Grandma Korolek, gasping again. "Look at the cake and the pony. There's even a band! Who did all this?"

"Many people helped," Nathan told her. "Bart the Baker made the cake. Grandma Pearson brought a pony from her farm. Mr. Gordon at the grocery store made the lunch. And Aunt Hazel brought the school band in her van."

"Who invited all the people?" asked Grandma Korolek.

"Miss Hossip at the newspaper told everyone to come," said Nathan. "Look at all the friends you have, Grandma Korolek."

"But it took a best friend to think of a surprise party. Thank you, Nathan!" said Grandma Korolek. She gave him a big hug.